JACQUELINE FER

The Falling Star

Interior Image Credit: Sulema Fernandez-Honn

ISBN: 978-1-7166-5945-4 (sc)
ISBN: 978-1-7166-5944-7 (e)

Lulu Publishing Services rev. date: 08/18/2020

The Falling Star

By Jacqueline Fernandez

Illustrated by Sulema Fernandez-Honn

Dedication

Dedicated to our beautiful stars in Heaven my mother Maria Fernandez and friend Carol Ratfield whose bright light will forever shine.

Acknowledgements

I would like to thank God in Heaven for his abounding grace. My family without whose love and help this book would never have been completed especially my little stars. Special thanks to friends and extended family who were very supportive during our difficult time.

Special appreciation for Sulema's beautiful illustrations that gave this book a visual narrative

Lastly, I would express Thanks to my wonderful father Heriberto Fernandez and also beloved friend Kenny Ratfield whose angels are watching them from Heaven.

La Lune the Moon has many children that are scattered throughout the sky.

They are dazzling jewels that light the sky at night.

It was rare... But it does happen that a star falls in love with a star that swims below, a starfish as they are known.

Gala a beautiful star that loves to dance in the sky like a diamond that shine so bright.

La Lune the Moon's cheerful child whose lovely nature brings happiness to those all around.

One day Gala the star that shined so bright heard a sweet song from the sea sung by a starfish that swam below a watery reef.

"Gala you are radiant with your sparkles. The twilight of the night leaving a dreamy silver glow for those in sight"

"I sing this sweet lullaby in hopes that you may come by and make this starfish heart soar like a kite on an afternoon flight."

The beautiful star had never looked below the glistening water where the beautiful colors flow.

The starfish was handsome that danced and swam in the watery mirror down on land. It was a kaleidoscope of shapes and colors that painted a lively pageant unlike no other.

"Your song has moved me starfish that swims below the sea. I do not understand why you would be so sad in the lively world of your land."

The starfish gazed upon Gala and with sad dismay spoke "I wish you could swim in the sea with me or that I could fly in the sky with you."

She twinkled with delight over such sweet words of might, expressed by the handsome starfish that swam on land.

He was silly to think in that way. "It could never be you see, we are different you and me. I fly in the sky and you swim in the sea."

The starfish smiled charmingly and spoke with sweet poetry. "I will not quarrel Gala. I am content you came and noticed me, I will wish every night for you to come and be with me. And know that true love conquers all.

Gala was enchanted by his words and soon felt it best to say adieu. A warm thought began to grow in her heart as she moved away from the starfish that blew a kiss her way.

She was lost in reverie from the words of the handsome starfish from the sea. La Lune the Moon heard the sweet melody for her child Gala and was amazed to see that love was growing between the star and starfish from the sea.

"Gala star of my delight that beams with such great light. Why are you sad my child?"

The star with tears tells her tale of sorrow to her beloved mother in the sky.

"The starfish that swims on land, his wish has come to plan. He said that true love conquers all. He wishes one day, not too far, to join him in the blue azure of his land. My heart belongs to the starfish from another land. I wish I may, I wish I might be with my starfish tonight."

La Lune the Moon kissed Gala goodnight and told her that her wish might come true tonight. Now true love does conquer but especially always remembering to show love and kindness to all.

The blue night saw a lovely jewel fall from the sky in a splendorous array of light, shooting millions of beams through the nocturnal night.

The world stood still as the sight was breathtaking for all to witness the beauty of the night.

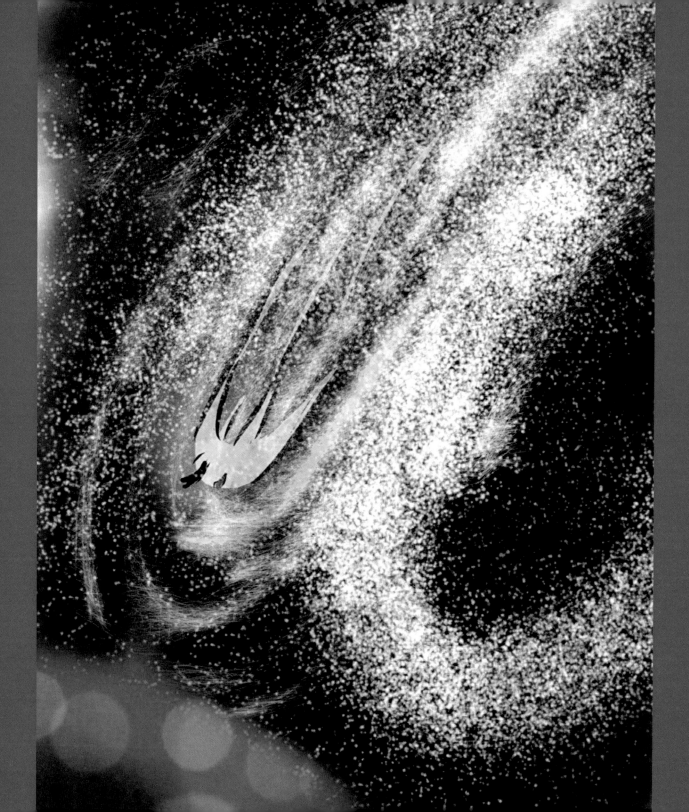

"I wish I may I wish I might make a wish tonight," was heard by La Lune the Moon. When a star does fall think of love, make a wish out loud and just maybe your dream will be heard!

The end